I AM READING

Creepy Customers

SAMANTHA HAY

ILLUSTRATED BY
SARAH WARBURTON

KINGFISHER

BOSTON

For Alice—S. H.

KINGFISHER
a Houghton Mifflin Company imprint
222 Berkeley Street
Boston, Massachusetts 02116
www.houghtonmifflinbooks.com

First published in 2005
2 4 6 8 10 9 7 5 3

LIBRARY OF CONGRESS CATALOGING-IN-PUBLICATION DATA
has been applied for.

ISBN 0-7534-5857-8
ISBN 978-07534-5857-0

Printed in Canada
2TR/0705/TCL/SGCH(SGCH)/80CAS/C

Contents

Chapter One
4

Chapter Two
13

Chapter Three
21

Chapter Four
29

Chapter Five
37

Chapter One

It was the first day of school vacation, and there were lots of exciting things that Steve could have been doing. He could have been skateboarding, climbing trees, or playing soccer. But he wasn't doing any of them.

Instead he was stuck inside his dad's dusty old pharmacy.

"I'm so bored!" he moaned.

"We haven't had a single customer all day."

"Well, look on the bright side," said Dad cheerfully. "It means that we've got plenty of time for our spring cleaning." And then he climbed his ladder to dust the top shelves.

Steve sighed. There had to be easier
ways to earn his allowance.
Just then the bell above the store
door rang.

A customer. At last! thought Steve.

It was an old woman dressed in black
wearing a pointy hat.

She looked like she was going to a
costume party—as a witch!

"Warts!" growled the old woman.

"Excuse me?" said Steve.

"Warts! I've got warts!"

She certainly did. They were all over
her nose.

Steve was wondering what she wanted
him to do about them, when Dad
called down from the ladder,
"Wart cream. Third shelf on the left."
Steve found it and put it in a bag.

"And shampoo!" barked the woman.
"I need shampoo for people with very
oily hair."

She certainly did. Her long black hair was greasy enough to cook fries in!

"The green bottle in the back," said Dad cheerfully.

"And I want lipstick, too!" ordered the woman. "Black lipstick!"

"Bottom shelf, next to the green eye shadow," called Dad.

Steve found it and took the old
woman's money.

She winked at Steve and shuffled off,
muttering to herself about finding a
store that sold snail saliva!

Snail saliva? thought Steve.

Chapter Two

Steve wanted to ask his dad what snail saliva was used for, but the bell above the door rang again.

It was another customer!

Except there wasn't anyone there.

That's odd, thought Steve.
Just then he felt a nip on
his ear.

"Yikes," he yowled.
Then he heard a
flutter of wings.

"Dad! I think there's a bird in the store."

Dad was still on his
ladder. "Mmm, it's
probably just a bat."

14

"Yes," said a voice. "Just a bat."
The voice belonged to a wrinkled old
man wearing a shiny black cape who
had suddenly appeared from nowhere.

"Bandages—I need an extra-big box,"
said the old man softly.

"Next to the soap," called Dad from
the top of his ladder.

"And I need toothpaste. Lots of toothpaste," he told Steve, revealing two long, sharp, pointy teeth.

Yikes, thought Steve.

The man looked a lot like a vampire.

"And stain remover," said the old man. "I have some troublesome bloodstains that won't come out." Steve shivered.

But he knew where the toothpaste and the stain remover were.

The man paid Steve for them.

Then suddenly Steve understood.

The costume party!

He was obviously going to the same one as the witch.

Steve smiled at the man.

"I like your costume."

The old man winked at Steve and then suddenly vanished.

Chapter Three

"Pass those tissues," said Steve's
dad from the top of his ladder.
Steve got the tissues. "I can't reach!"
"Maybe I can help?"
Steve turned to see the biggest and
hairiest man that he'd ever seen.

Actually, he looked more like a wolf
than a man.

As the man passed the tissues
to Dad, Steve had a good, long
look at him.

He had hair everywhere.

It sprouted from his cuffs,

the collar of
his shirt,

and even out
of his ears.

"I need some nail clippers,"
said the man in a deep,
growly voice.

He certainly did. His nails looked like
claws—long, pointy, and very dirty.

"Next to the nail polish," called
down Dad.

Steve swallowed hard. The hairy man
had a tail!

"And an extra-strong comb!"
"Over by the shampoo," said Dad.

Of course! He was going to the same costume party as the witch and the vampire.

He was supposed to be a werewolf!

"You really do look like one, you know," said Steve when he took the man's money.

TRIAL PRICE!

The man winked at him and then trotted out of the store.

Chapter Four

I wish I could go to a costume party, thought Steve. *It would be much better than being stuck in this boring old store.* Just then there was a thundering sound outside.

"Dad, I think there's a storm coming."

"Mmm, maybe," said his dad.

"Or maybe it's just a horse."

Steve peered out of the store window.

It was a horse.

But not like any horse that Steve

had ever seen before.

Big and black, it had wild eyes and
steam coming out of its nostrils.
Its rider swung himself out of the
saddle and flung open the door.
Steve was almost knocked over
by the gust of wind that came
with him.

The man was tall and thin and
shrouded in black.
Steve couldn't even see his face.

"Cough drops," he gasped from under his hood.

"Second aisle," called Dad from the top of his ladder.

"Extra-strong," gasped the voice.

Steve still couldn't see his head.

And then he did.

It was tucked under the man's arm!

"ARRRRGH!" yelled Steve.

He was so surprised that he dropped the cough drops.

But then he guessed.

"Of course," he said. "You must be the headless horseman. You're going to the costume party too!"

The head smirked but said nothing.

"I love your costume. How do you do that thing with your head?" asked Steve.

"Let me show you," rasped the head.

He pulled back his hood and revealed . . .

Nothing!

There was no head there, just a stumpy neck.

"ARRRRGH!" screamed Steve.

Chapter Five

The headless horseman's head winked at Steve from under his arm, and then he turned and left the store, clutching his cough drops.

"I hope he paid for them," said Dad from the top of his ladder.

Steve was stunned.

"Dad, that man didn't have a head!

Well, at least not attached to his body!"

"As I always tell you, Steve," said his dad, climbing down from his ladder. "There's always someone worse off than you."

Steve could see his point.

Suddenly, he had a thought. If the headless horseman *was* real, then the others might be too.

Maybe the old woman *was* a witch.

Maybe the old man *was* a vampire.

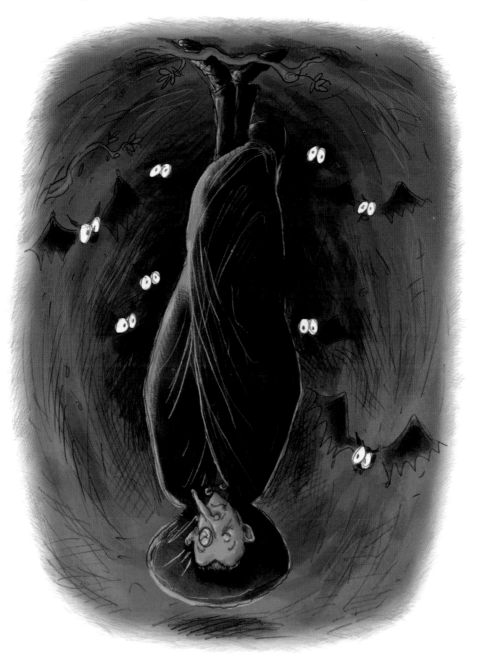

And the hairy wolf man might
actually *be* a real werewolf.

Steve felt his knees begin to knock.

"Okay, I'm finished," said his dad.
"You can go out and play now if you want."

"Play?" said Steve. "I don't want to go out and play!"

"Ah!" said Dad. "So, working here isn't as boring as you thought?"

"Boring?" said Steve. "No way!"

He was about to
tell his dad all about
the creepy customers
that he'd served
when he noticed that
his dad was grinning.
"You know, Steve,
there's never a dull
moment when you
run a store! You
never know who—
or what—your next
customer might be!"

45

He gave Steve an extra-big wink and went behind the counter, chuckling softly to himself.

About the author and illustrator

Samantha Hay comes from Scotland. For the past ten years she has worked in television, but she is currently

taking time off to look after her little girl and write stories. *Creepy Customers* is her first book to be published. "My big brother always tells me I look a bit like a vampire," says Sam. "My skin is quite white, and I love red lipstick! So fancy dress [costume] parties aren't a problem for me!"

Sarah Warburton was born in north Wales but now lives in Bristol, England, with her husband. She has been illustrating books for more than ten years. Sarah says, "As a girl I would always go to Halloween parties as a witch. However, I don't think I'd enjoy being a real witch, as I'm terrified of spiders and allergic to cats! Witches are great fun to draw, though, as they're mostly ugly, mean, and warty!"

Strategies for Independent Readers

Predict
Think about the cover, illustrations, and the title of the book. What do you think this book will be about? While you are reading think about what may happen next and why.

Monitor
As you read ask yourself if what you're reading makes sense. If it doesn't, reread, look at the illustrations, or read ahead.

Question
Ask yourself questions about important ideas in the story such as what the characters might do or what you might learn.

Phonics
If there is a word that you do not know, look carefully at the letters, sounds, and word parts that you do know. Blend the sounds to read the word. Ask yourself if this is a word you know. Does it make sense in the sentence?

Summarize
Think about the characters, the setting where the story takes place, and the problem the characters faced in the story. Tell the important ideas in the beginning, middle, and end of the story.

Evaluate
Ask yourself questions like: Did you like the story? Why or why not? How did the author make the story come alive? How did the author make the story fun to read? How well did you understand the story? Maybe you can understand it better if you read it again!